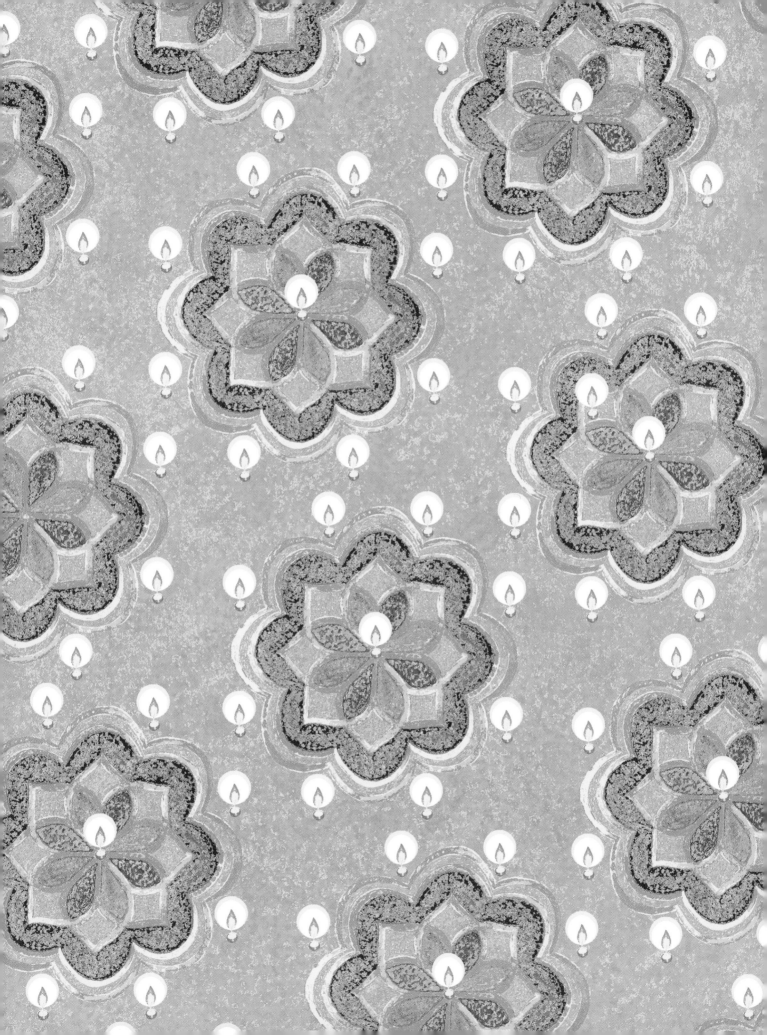

*To Keegan Nolan*
—GLORIA

*For RW*
*For your high expectations—always.*
—AMANDA

Text Copyright © 2013 Gloria Whelan
Illustrations Copyright © 2013 Amanda Hall

## Sleeping Bear Press™

315 East Eisenhower Parkway, Suite 200
Ann Arbor, MI 48108
www.sleepingbearpress.com
© Sleeping Bear Press

Printed and bound in the United States.
10 9 8 7 6 5 4 3 2 1

Library of Congress Cataloging-in-Publication Data

Whelan, Gloria.
In Andal's house / written by Gloria Whelan ; illustrated by Amanda Hall.
p. cm.
Summary: "Kumar, a young boy living in present-day India, faces bigotry
when he goes to visit a classmate from a higher caste family"- Provided by the publisher.
ISBN 978-1-58536-603-3
[1. Prejudices–Fiction. 2. Social classes–Fiction. 3. India–Fiction.]
I. Hall, Amanda, ill. II. Title.
PZ7.W5718Imt 2013
[Fic]–dc23
2012033684

# IN ANDAL'S HOUSE

Gloria Whelan

Illustrated by Amanda Hall

Tales of the World *from* Sleeping Bear Press

**INDIA**

Kumar's mother gave him another helping of mango pickle to go with his dal. "Are you sure you are invited to Andal's house?" she asked.

"I'm sure," Kumar insisted. "It's just for the fireworks."

"I would not invite my son's friends into my home without giving them a proper meal, especially on a holiday like Diwali. When a guest walks into your house, God comes with him and there must be food waiting."

Anika said, "The family is high-caste Brahmin and very wealthy. Maybe they do things differently."

"No," Kumar told his older sister, "in school Andal is not stuck-up. He is a friend with everybody in our fourth class."

❧

That was not exactly true. Only some of the class had been invited to Andal's house to see the fireworks and Kumar was pleased that although his family had little money, he had been one of the lucky ones.

Kumar's father always stuck up for Kumar and now said, "The boy knows what he was told."

His grandfather said nothing, which was unlike him, for he had an opinion on everything. He only frowned and tore his chapati in an angry way.

When dinner was finished Kumar was sent out to light the oil in the clay Diwali lamps along the path to their house. Just outside of the door he stepped carefully over the rangoli his sister had made that day. The rice flour design was very beautiful with its red-and-green pattern of the lotus flower.

It made Kumar feel guilty, for Anika was a talented artist and longed to go to the National Institute of Design in their city. Instead she was working in the textile factory earning money so that one day Kumar might go to the university. The little money his father made as a postal worker would not be enough for tuition.

His family wanted Kumar to become a doctor or a lawyer, but secretly Kumar wanted to work at the Tata Motors and make cars. The streets were full of the little orange and yellow automobiles. Or maybe he would be a computer programmer or a famous cricket player and play for India.

Knowing the sacrifice his sister was making, Kumar
worked hard at his studies. He knew English and Hindi and
Gujarati, the language of his state of Gujarat. He was the
best student in his class and he believed that was why Andal
invited him to his fireworks party.

It was time to walk the five blocks to Andal's home. At first his mother had wanted Anika to walk with him, but Kumar had rebelled.

"How can I turn up in front of my friends like a little dog tied to my sister's leash?"

"Let the boy go on his own," his father said.

Half in fun, but also to let his sister know he cared for her, Kumar bent to touch his sister's feet, for all women carried the holiness of the feminine goddess within themselves.

⚜

Kumar set off in his new shirt and new shorts purchased for Diwali. On his feet were the trainers like Andal's that he had coaxed his mother to buy. He knew that because of the trainers Anika would have to wait for the new dress she needed. He resolved to work even harder at school. If he earned a scholarship Anika could take the money she was saving for him and go to the design school or put it aside for her dowry so that one day she could be married.

The humid monsoon rains were gone and the November
evening was pleasantly cool. The city looked to Kumar as if
there had been an invasion of giant fireflies.

Diwali lamps sparkled everywhere. Fireworks made dazzling patterns in the sky. The whole town was aglow.

The streets were crowded with holiday shoppers, all in a good mood. You could bump into someone and they only laughed and wished you well. The women in their saris were like brightly colored butterflies. Doorways were decorated with garlands of mango leaves and marigolds. Stores' windows displayed jewelry to be given as Diwali gifts. Peddlers were selling every kind of sweet, including his favorite, malpuas, the little fried balls flavored with coconut and bananas.

Kumar paused outside of Andal's house. His home could
fit into that of Andal's many times. He had never been in the
home of a high-caste Brahmin.

His own family had been outcasts, having no caste at all.
*Untouchables*, they were once called. All that was in the past.
People had forgotten such things.

A servant opened the door and led Kumar into a hallway.
Over the servant's shoulder Kumar could see into a room
where Andal and the other boys were gathered. He recognized
two friends from his class, Manit and Janu. Like Andal the
boys were Brahmin.

As Kumar set off to join the others a white-haired lady hurried
up to him. Kumar decided she must be Andal's grandmother.
He thought Andal was lucky to have a grandmother. His own
grandmother had died a year ago and he missed her.

The grandmother said, "You are Kumar." She stood between him and the room of boys.

"Yes, Ma'am," Kumar said. "I have come to see the fireworks."

"I am very sorry but you cannot stay. Andal was wrong to invite you. I do not mean to be unkind, but we cannot have a boy of no caste in our home. It would never do."

She signaled to the servant, who led Kumar to the door.

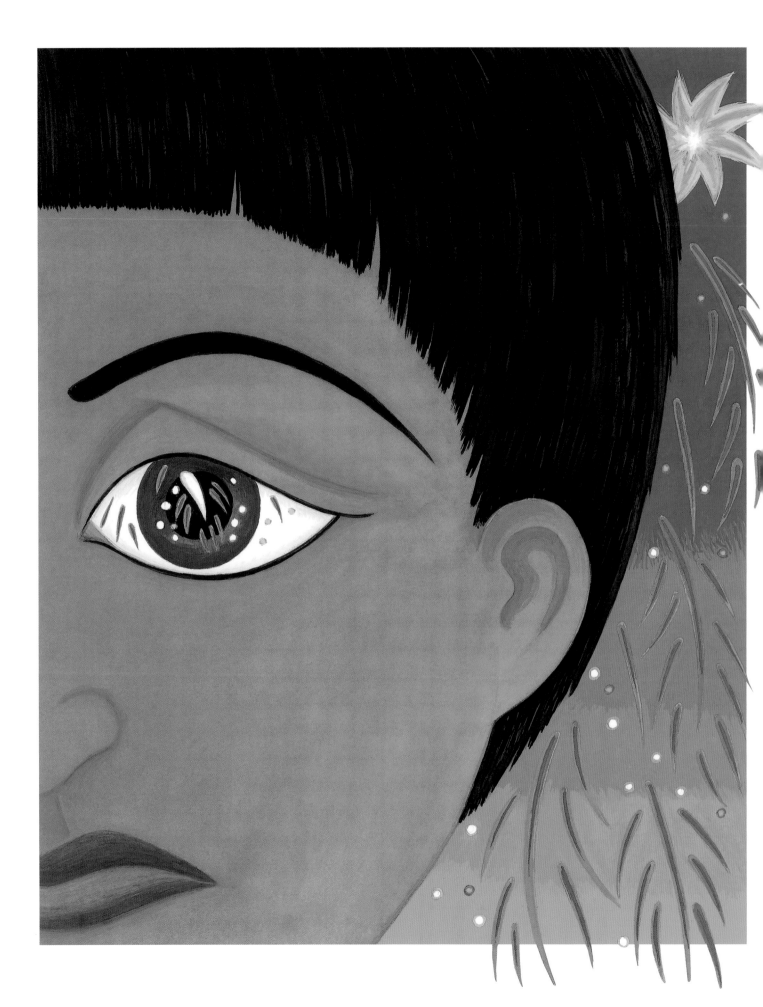

As Kumar walked home fireworks exploded in brilliant patterns of stars and fountains and pinwheels. He had been looking forward all week to watching them with Andal and the other boys. Now they were spoiled for him. He watched them fall to the ground like brightly colored tears.

When Kumar arrived back at his house, only his grandfather was at home. His parents and Anika had not yet returned from the public fireworks. Kumar told his grandfather what had happened at Andal's house.

"Nothing has changed," Kumar said. "It is just as bad for us outcasts as it always was."

"No, Kumar," his grandfather said, "it is not as it always was. At your age the only job I could get was that of a sweeper, cleaning the streets of dirt and what the cows left. I was an untouchable. I had to shout, 'Posh, posh, sweeper coming,' to warn people so that they could hurry out of my way. They believed even my shadow was unclean. If it fell upon someone, they had to bathe to cleanse themselves. They called after me, 'Dirty dog,' and worse."

"I could not draw water for my mother from the well lest I pollute the well. I had to beg water from others. If I was given a drink of water, it was from a clay cup and afterward the cup was broken. I could not go into a store. There was no school for me. To this day I cannot read or write very well.

"The great man, Gandhi, said such treatment of the untouchables was very wrong. He called us *Harijans*, children of God. Then came Dr. Ambedkar who called us the *Dalit*, the broken people. All his life he fought for our rights. Today the government outlaws such discrimination. Under the law, Kumar, we are all equal."

"Not in Andal's house," Kumar said. "Why should I work hard if I am to be despised because of something I can't help?"

"Look out of the window, Kumar. There are lights all over the city. We light the lamps of Diwali to drive away the darkness of ignorance. In Andal's house you have both the past and the future. Among older people like Andal's grandmother we will always be untouchables, but foolish and unkind people should not rule our lives. Your friend, Andal, does not think like that, and you will be living not in his grandmother's world but in Andal's world, which is *your* world as well."

Kumar was awake long after Anika and his parents came home. Everyone in the house was asleep and still Kumar stood at the window, watching as one by one the Diwali lights went out all over the city. At last he went to sleep. Another night would come and once again the lamps would light up the darkness.

**Brahmin**: the highest Hindu caste

**caste**: a social rank or division into which Hindu society is divided

**chapati**: an unleavened flatbread

**cricket**: similar to baseball, a game played with a ball and bat and eleven players on each side

**dal**: a spiced sauce of pureed lentils

**Dalit**: the name given to the outcasts or untouchables by Dr. Ambedkar. In the Sanskrit language the word means "broken to pieces."

**Diwali**: an official five-day holiday celebrated in India. Also called "Festival of Lights." There are fireworks and the lighting of little clay lamps, a symbol of the victory of light and goodness over darkness and evil.

**Doctor Ambedkar**: an Indian political leader who fought against the caste system and all forms of social discrimination

**dowry**: a gift given by the family of a bride to the family of the groom

**Mohandas Gandhi**: India's greatest spiritual and political leader who, employing nonviolence, worked for India's independence and led the fight for the poor, for women's rights, and against the caste system

**Harijan**: "Children of God," Gandhi's name for the untouchables

**malpuas**: deep-fried pancakes flavored with a sweet sauce

**monsoon**: a storm with powerful wind and rain that occurs from June through October

**rangoli**: an ancient art of India, and a Diwali tradition, where colored powders, grains, or beads are used to form designs on floors or sidewalks

**sari**: a long length of cloth, wrapped to make a skirt and then draped over the shoulder and the head

**Tata Motors**: India's largest automobile company

**trainers**: sneakers

**untouchable**: outcast. The untouchables had no designated caste and were relegated to do the jobs no one else wanted to do.

# AUTHOR'S NOTE

When I was writing the novel about India, *Homeless Bird*,
I briefly mentioned the *untouchables*, the Indians who
belonged to no caste, and who for centuries have been
the victims of discrimination. I continued to think about
them and I followed their misfortunes and, more happily,
their fortunes as the prejudices of the past fell away. They
began to be welcome in schools and universities where

scholarships were available to them. A president of India and a chief law minister have come from the untouchable castes. I wanted to tell the story of how much has been achieved and how there still remains more to accomplish. It is a story that could be told not only about India, but also about any country where a class of people have been denied the right to be all they can be.

—Gloria Whelan

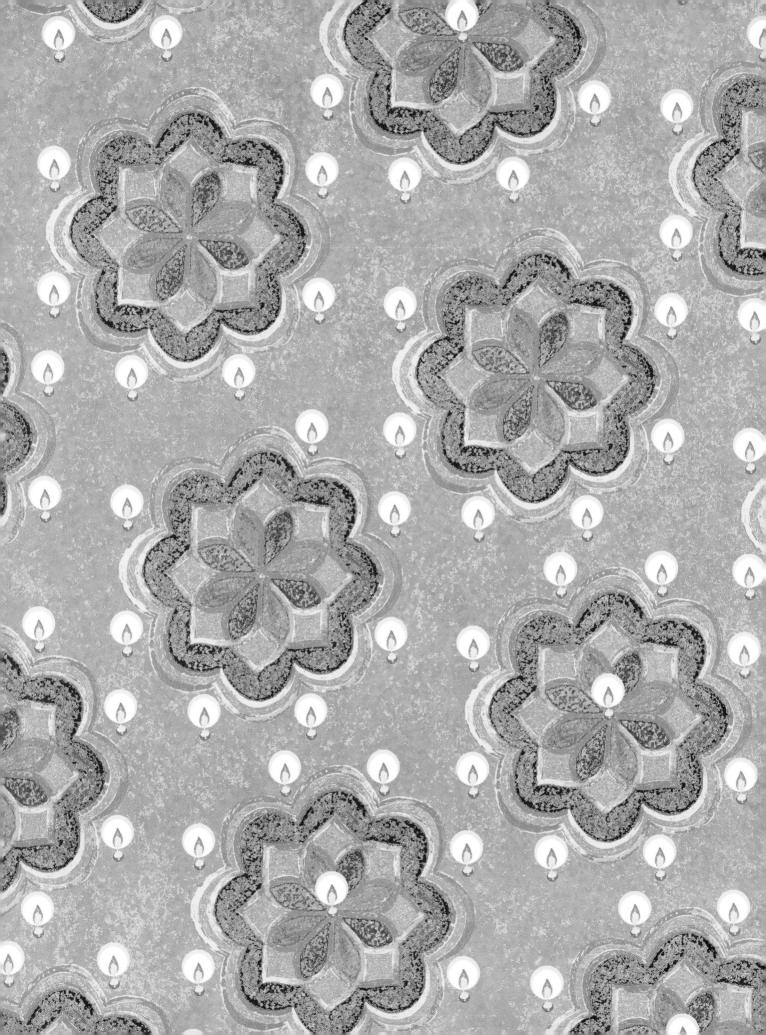